Clifford THE BIG RED DOG ®

THE BIG ITCH

Adapted by Alison Inches
From the television script "An Itchy Patch"
by Anne-Marie Perrotta and Tean Schultz
Illustrated by Robbin Cuddy

**Based on the Scholastic book series
"Clifford The Big Red Dog"
by Norman Bridwell**

One day Clifford had a big itch.

He scratched it against everything.

He scratched it against an apple tree.

"Clifford!" said Samuel and Ms. Lee.

He scratched it against a stoplight.

"Clifford!" said the bus driver.

He scratched it against Mr. Carson's truck.

"Clifford!" said Mr. Carson.

At home, Clifford scratched . . .

and scratched . . .

and scratched!

"If he keeps scratching," said

Emily Elizabeth's dad,

"he will have to go to the vet."

The vet? thought Clifford.

Clifford had never been to the

new vet before.

Clifford ran to the beach

and told his friends.

"Trust me," said Cleo,

"you do *not* want to go to the vet."

"What should I do?" asked Clifford.

"Stop scratching," said Cleo. "No

scratching—no vet!"

At the library, Clifford tried not

to scratch.

But he was *so* itchy!

He rolled over and over.

Ms. Lee looked out the window.

"Wow," she said.

"Clifford sure has a big itch."

"Clifford!" cried Emily.

"Are you scratching again?"

Clifford pretended to play.

So did Cleo and T-Bone.

"You were just playing?"

Emily Elizabeth asked.

"Woof!" they barked together.

Emily Elizabeth had lunch at Samuel's Fish and Chips.

"How is Clifford's itch?" asked Samuel.

"I haven't seen him scratch all day," said Emily Elizabeth.

They looked out at Clifford.

He looked happy.

And he *was* happy.

Cleo and T-Bone were scratching his back!

"That feels so good!" said Clifford.

But soon Cleo and T-Bone got tired of scratching.

Clifford's big itch got bigger and bigger!

Clifford ran down the beach.

He jumped into the water.

He rubbed his back on the ferry dock.

"Clifford!" cried Emily Elizabeth.

Clifford looked up.

"It's time to go to the vet," she said.

"Dr. Dihn will take care of you."

Clifford whined.

"It will be okay, " said Emily Elizabeth.

"You'll see."

The whole family drove to the vet.

"You must be Clifford!" said Dr. Dihn.

She checked his back.

"I have some cream that will fix that

rash," said Dr. Dihn.

"Poor Clifford. He's all alone

at the vet's office," said Cleo.

"He's not alone," said T-Bone.

"Emily Elizabeth is with him.

And she would never let anyone hurt him."

Dr. Dihn spread the cream on

Clifford's back.

Clifford felt all better.

He howled with joy.

Everyone cheered for Clifford.

Clifford wagged his tail.

He gave Dr. Dihn a big kiss.

"Oh, my!" she said.

"I think you've made a friend

for life!" Emily Elizabeth said.

"Dr. Dihn took good care of you," said

Emily Elizabeth.

"And I will always take good care of you.

Because you are Clifford, my Big Red Dog!"

Do You Remember?

Circle the right answer.

1. Where was Clifford's itch?
    a. On his head.
    b. On his back.
    c. On his tummy.

2. At the beach, what did Clifford scratch against?
    a. The ferry dock.
    b. A rowboat.
    c. A beach chair.

Which happened first?

Which happened next?

Which happened last?

Write a 1, 2, or 3 in the space after each sentence.

Clifford scratched against Mr. Carson's truck. _____

Clifford went to the library with Emily. _____

Clifford scratched against an apple tree. _____

Answers:

Clifford scratched against an apple tree. (1)
Clifford went to the library with Emily. (3)
Clifford scratched against Mr. Carson's truck. (2)
2. a
1. b

Clifford THE BIG RED DOG®

THE BIG WHITE GHOST

Adapted by Gail Herman
From the television script "Boo!" by Lois Becker and Mark Stratton
Illustrated by Ken Edwards

**Based on the Scholastic book series
"Clifford The Big Red Dog"
by Norman Bridwell**

It was Halloween night

on Birdwell Island.

Everyone was going to the beach.

They were going to see

a spooky movie.

"Grrr!" A scary monster ran up to Clifford. Clifford backed away. Then he saw it was Mac.

"That was scary!" said Clifford.

"Nothing scares Jetta and me," Mac said.

"Not even T-Bone?" asked Cleo.

"Not even the Ghost Dog of Birdwell Island?" T-Bone asked.

A ghost dog?

Clifford's fur stood on end.

But Mac only laughed.

"There's no such thing as ghosts," he said.

The movie was about to begin.

Emily Elizabeth patted Clifford.

"He has never seen a movie,"

she told Jetta.

"And this is a spooky one!"

"Nothing scares us,"

Jetta said. "Right, Mac?"

A ghost appeared

on the movie screen.

Clifford gasped.

Jetta and Mac yawned.

Clifford hid his eyes

for the whole movie.

Finally, he peeked out.

Emily Elizabeth was clapping.

The movie was over.

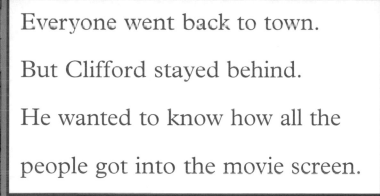

Everyone went back to town.

But Clifford stayed behind.

He wanted to know how all the

people got into the movie screen.

Clifford looked at the screen.

It was just a big white sheet.

The wind blew. *Whoosh!*

The sheet flapped.

The wind blew harder. *Whoosh!*

The sheet blew free.

It dropped over Clifford.

Clifford whirled around . . .

. . . and around.

What was going on?

Now he was very scared!

"That movie was fun,"

said Emily Elizabeth.

"And it was scary!"

"Humph!" said Jetta.

"It didn't scare me one bit!"

"But it's fun to be scared on

Halloween," said Emily Elizabeth.

"I've had enough of Halloween,"

said Jetta.

"Mac and I are going home."

A few minutes later,

Jetta and Mac ran back.

"Help! There's a ghost!"

Jetta yelled. "Run!"

"It's big! It's white!

And it's coming this way!"

Jetta shouted.

Boom! Crash!

Something was out there.

And it was coming closer.

"It's the Ghost Dog

of Birdwell Island!"

Mac cried.

Everyone hid.

Only Emily Elizabeth stood still.

The big white ghost

came closer . . .

and closer. . . .

Emily Elizabeth stuck out
her foot.
The sheet covering Clifford
slid off.

"Why, it's not a big white ghost," said T-Bone.

"It's a Big Red Dog!" Cleo said.

"It's okay," Emily Elizabeth told

Clifford. "I'm right here."

But where were Jetta and Mac?

They were hiding
under the table!
"Everyone gets
scared sometimes,"
Emily Elizabeth told Jetta.
"Even big brave dogs
like Mac and Clifford."

"Maybe next year, Clifford can wear a sheet for Halloween," Emily Elizabeth said.

"Then he will really be Clifford, my big white ghost!"

Clifford wagged his tail.

That wasn't scary at all.

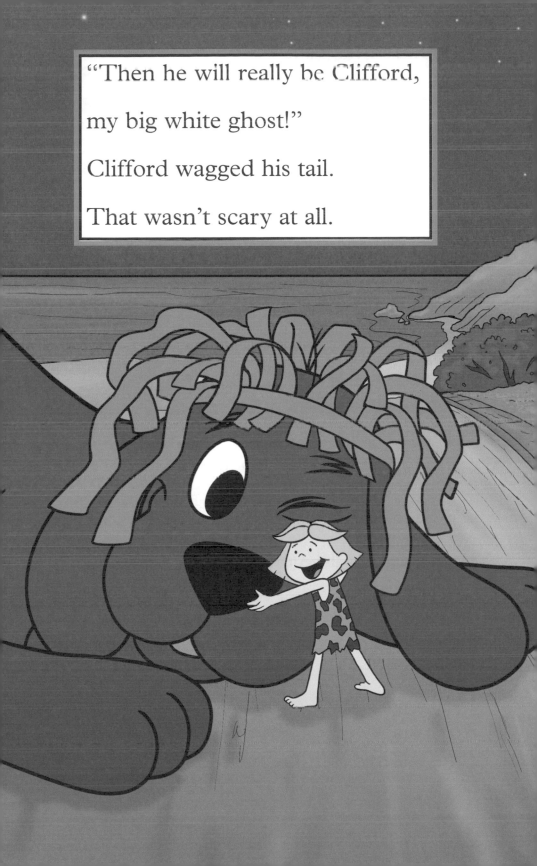

Do You Remember?

Circle the right answer.

1. Emily Elizabeth took Clifford to a movie . . .
   a. at a movie theater.
   b. at school.
   c. at the beach.

2. Why did Clifford look like a ghost?
   a. Mac played a trick on him.
   b. A white sheet fell on him.
   c. It was his Halloween costume.

Which happened first?
Which happened next?
Which happened last?
Write a 1, 2, or 3 in the space after each sentence.

The sheet falls on Clifford. _____

Everyone watches the movie. _____

Mac scares Clifford. _____

Answers:

Mac scares Clifford. (1)
Everyone watches the movie. (2)
The sheet falls on Clifford. (3)
2. b
1. c

Clifford THE BIG RED DOG ®
THE MYSTERY
OF THE
KIBBLE CROOK

Adapted by Liz Mills

Illustrated by Gita Lloyd and Eric Binder

Based on the Scholastic book series
"Clifford The Big Red Dog"
by Norman Bridwell

From the television script "Kibble Crook"
by Dev Ross

One day, T-Bone ran into Cleo's yard.

"Clifford! Cleo! Let's play!"

he shouted.

But no one was there.

T-Bone lay down on the grass to wait.

Then he saw Cleo's bowl.

And he smelled something good.

"I'll ask Cleo if I can try

her dog food when she gets back,"

said T-Bone.

But the longer he waited,

the better the food smelled.

T-Bone thought he would

just have a little taste.

"Wow! This food is great!"

said T-Bone.

And he took another taste.

T-Bone ate more and more…

until it was all gone!

"Oh, no!" he cried.

"I ate all of Cleo's food!

She's going to be so mad!

What am I going to tell her?"

Then Clifford, Cleo, and Mac

walked into the yard.

"I want everyone to try

my new dog food," said Cleo.

"Oh, no!" she cried.

"What's wrong?" asked Clifford.

"Somebody ate my food!" she shouted.

"Maybe a kibble crook took it,"
said Mac. "That's what you call a dog
who eats another dog's food."

Cleo turned to T-Bone.

"Did you see anyone?" she asked.

T-Bone was afraid to tell the truth.

"I think I saw a dog run down the street," he said.

"Which way did he go?" Cleo asked.

"I think he ran toward the dock,"

T-Bone said.

"Let's go make him say he's sorry!"

said Mac.

The dogs ran off.

At the dock, the dogs sniffed right.

They sniffed left.

They looked high.

They looked low.

No kibble crook.

T-Bone stopped to scratch his ear.

"They are not going to find anything.

I'm the kibble crook," he thought sadly.

T-Bone scratched harder.

He bumped into a box next to him.

Then he heard a noise.

Bark! Bark! Bark!

It came from inside the box.

The other dogs ran over.

"That sounds like a dog to me!"
said Mac.

"Yeah," said Cleo, "and I bet it's
stuffed with my kibble!"

Clifford turned over the box with
his paw.

Lots of toy dogs were inside, barking.

"Well, Cleo, they're stuffed, but not
with your kibble!" said Clifford.

"Maybe we should give up.

It's only dog food," said T-Bone.

"That dog ate *my* kibble without

asking!" said Cleo.

"Oh, yeah," said T-Bone.

The dogs walked toward the beach.

Mac stopped in front of a cave.

"Every crook needs a hideout," he said. "This cave is perfect!"

Clifford walked up to the cave.

"Hellooooo!" he shouted.

"Hellooooo!" came an echo.

"It's the kibble crook!"

whispered Cleo.

"Let's go catch him!" said Mac.

"Wait!" T-Bone said. "I don't think you should go in there."

"Why not?" asked Clifford.

"Because I'm the one who…who…"

T-Bone stopped.

He looked at the ground.

"What?" asked Mac.

"Because I'm the one who
should go in there by myself,"
said T-Bone.

"That's very brave of you," said
Clifford. "Are you sure you don't
want us to come with you?"

T-Bone nodded sadly.

He walked into the cave.

After a while, Clifford started walking back and forth. "Clifford," asked Cleo, "will you stop doing that?"

"But I'm worried about T-Bone,"
said Clifford.

Inside the cave, T-Bone thought about
how he ate Cleo's new dog food.
He thought about how he told a lie to
his friends.

And then he walked out
of the cave.

"Did you catch him, T-Bone?" asked Cleo.

"There is no kibble crook. *I* ate your new dog food, Cleo," said T-Bone. "I'm sorry."

"Why didn't you say so before?" asked Cleo.

"I was afraid you'd be mad at me," said T-Bone. "But I promise to always tell the truth from now on."

Cleo smiled. "Okay. Let's see if there's more dog food at home!" And the dogs ran off together.

Do You Remember?

Circle the right answer.

1. Who ate Cleo's food?
   - a. The seagulls
   - b. Mac
   - c. T-Bone

2. Near the beach, Mac found...
   - a. a treasure.
   - b. a cave.
   - c. an anchor.

Which happened first?
Which happened next?
Which happened last?
Write a 1, 2, or 3 in the space after each sentence.

T-Bone told the truth.   _____

Cleo's food bowl was empty.   _____

The dogs searched the dock.   _____

Answers:

The dogs searched the dock. (2)
Cleo's food bowl was empty. (1)
T-Bone told the truth. (3)
2. b
1. c

Clifford THE BIG RED DOG ®

THE BIG
BAD COLD

Adapted by Liz Mills from the
television script "Get Well" by Don Gilles
Illustrated by Carolyn Bracken & Ken Edwards

**Based on the Scholastic book series
"Clifford The Big Red Dog"
by Norman Bridwell**

Clifford was waiting for Emily Elizabeth.

T-Bone and Cleo were waiting with him.

They wanted her to come out and play.

Clifford looked in the window.

"Oh, Clifford," Emily Elizabeth said.

"I can't come out today.

I have a bad cold."

"AH-CHOO!"

"What was that?" asked T-Bone.

"Who was that?" asked Cleo.

"It's Emily Elizabeth," said Clifford.

"She's got a bad cold. Poor Emily."

"I know what will make her feel
better," said T-Bone.
"Get-well gifts!"

"We can make her a get-well card!"
Clifford said.

"We can give her a big balloon!" said Cleo.

"We can give her a bunch of flowers!"
T-Bone said.

"And I know just where to find some."

"These flowers are just right, T-Bone,"

said Clifford.

"Uh-oh. Stop, Clifford. Stop!" cried T-Bone.

All the flower tops floated away.

"Sorry," said Clifford.

"That's all right," said T-Bone.

"The flowers look different," Cleo said,

"but they're still pretty."

"Right!" Clifford said.

"Emily Elizabeth will like them."

"We still need a card and a balloon,"

said Cleo.

They walked over to the pier.

"Hey, look at that!" Cleo said.

Samuel was standing in front

of the Fish-and-Chips Shack.

"Free balloons today!" he called.

"Come and get your free balloon!"

Cleo ran to the balloons.

She tried to get one.

She jumped—and the next

thing she knew . . .

. . . she was floating up, up, and away!

Clifford and T-Bone ran after her.

At last, the balloons caught on a flagpole.

Clifford helped Cleo get down.

"How about just one balloon, Cleo?"
said Samuel.

Cleo barked.

"I'll take that as a 'yes,'" Samuel said.
He laughed and tied a yellow balloon
to Cleo's tail.

"I'm glad you're okay, Cleo," said Clifford.

"That's a great balloon!"

Just then, Clifford stepped on

something that was lying on the sidewalk.

"This piece of cardboard would be perfect

for Emily Elizabeth's card," he said.

"But look—I spoiled it!"

"Don't worry, Clifford," said Cleo.

"T-Bone and I will fix it up."

"This is like finger painting, but

I call it body painting!" said T-Bone.

"Looks great!" Cleo said.

"Just one more little spot, right here!"

"Perfect!" said Clifford.

"Emily Elizabeth will love it!"

Suddenly, the wind blew the card

over the fence—

right into the Bleakmans' yard!

"Remember—the Bleakmans said we can't go into their yard," Clifford said.

"Not even one paw."

"Then we'll have to get the card some other way," said Cleo.

"Swing T-Bone one more time, Clifford,"

said Cleo.

"He just has to grab the card in his teeth.

You can do it, T-Bone!"

T-Bone went flying, back and forth.

Luckily, Mr. Bleakman didn't see him.

T-Bone went lower and lower.

"You've got it, T-Bone!" said Cleo.

"Yay, T-Bone!" Clifford cheered.

"You did it!"

At last, the dogs were ready

to give Emily Elizabeth her gifts.

"Are these for me?" Emily Elizabeth asked.

"Thank you all!

I feel better already!

I have the best friends in the world."

Do You Remember?

Circle the right answer.

1. Who gave Emily Elizabeth a bunch of flowers?
    a. Mr. Bleakman
    b. Cleo
    c. T-Bone

2. Clifford's gift to Emily was . . .
    a. a candy bar
    b. a big card
    c. a toy

Which happened first?
Which happened next?
Which happened last?
Write a 1, 2, or 3 in the space after each sentence.

1. Samuel tied a balloon
to Cleo's tail.   _____

2. Emily Elizabeth was in
bed with a cold.   _____

3. The wind blew the card into
the Bleakmans' yard.   _____

Answers:

(3) The wind blew the card into the Bleakmans' yard.
(1) Emily Elizabeth was in bed with a cold.
(2) Samuel tied a balloon to Cleo's tail.
2. b
1. c

WINTER ICE IS NICE!

Adapted by Bob Barkly
From the television script "That's Snow Lie" by Scott Guy
Illustrated by Carolyn Bracken & Ken Edwards

**Based on the Scholastic book series
"Clifford The Big Red Dog"
by Norman Bridwell**

It was winter on

Birdwell Island.

Emily Elizabeth and her

friends were playing

in the snow.

"Look out!" Charley yelled.

"Here I come!"

He went flying down the hill.

Clifford and his friends

were at the soccer field.

It was covered with ice.

"Look at me!" T-Bone said.

"I'll show you my famous

Hop, Hop, and Slide."

T-Bone ran fast.

He hopped high . . .

. . . and he slid across the ice!

"Watch me!"
Mac said.
"Hop, hop—
and slide!"

Clifford was next.

He took one hop. . . .

Oops!

He hopped too far!

Clifford began again.

But this time he went

right to the sliding part.

"Whee!" Clifford said.

"Whoa!" said T-Bone.

Clifford stopped just in time!

"That was great!" Clifford said.

"Now you go, Cleo!"

"Uh, um, okay," Cleo said.

"Here I come."

Cleo took one little step. . .

. . . and down she went.

Clifford, Mac, and T-Bone

came over.

"Are you okay?"

Clifford asked.

"Um . . . well . . . I think

I hurt my paw, " Cleo said.

"Maybe we should get Dr. Dihn,"

said T-Bone.

"No!" Cleo yelled.

"I just need to rest my paw."

Clifford made a place for Cleo

to rest.

"A snow couch!" she said. "Cool!"

Mac kept sliding. He was having fun.

Later, Clifford gave Cleo

a ride home.

"Thanks, Clifford," she said.

Cleo limped up to her house.

"Hey, Cleo," T-Bone said.

"I thought it was your

other paw that hurt."

Cleo stopped.

"Uh, um, " she said.

"Oh, no! It must be spreading!

Both my paws hurt now.

I have to go in

and lie down."

The next day Clifford,

Mac, and T-Bone went

back to Cleo's house.

Cleo was playing in the yard.

"Do you want to come skate

with us?" Clifford asked.

Cleo stopped playing.

 "I don't know," she said.

"My paw still hurts."

"I thought it was your *front*

paw that hurt," Mac said.

"Huh? Oh, yeah," Cleo said.

"But don't worry.

I can still watch."

"It's funny how Cleo's sore paw keeps moving around," T-Bone said.

"Sure is," Mac said.

At the ice rink, Clifford

spun around and around

on his big red tail.

"Come on, guys," he said.

"This is fun."

T-Bone ran onto the ice.

But Mac stayed behind.

"I don't know how

to do that," he said.

"I'll look silly."

"Who cares?" Clifford said.

"No one does it perfect

the first time. Try it," he said.

"Okay, I'll try," Mac said.

Mac flipped and he flopped.

But soon he could spin

as fast as Clifford and T-Bone.

Cleo jumped up on all fours.

"That does look like fun,"

she said.

Suddenly, she lifted up her paw.

"Maybe your paw is better now,"

Clifford said to her.

"You know, I think you're right!"

Cleo said.

She ran to the ice.

Cleo spun around.

"Wheeee!" she cried.

"What about your sore paw?"

Mac said.

Cleo looked down.

"I didn't really hurt my
paw," she said. "I never
skated before. I was afraid
you guys would think I look silly."

"But trying new things

with your friends

is fun," Clifford said.

"And so is being silly."

"You're right!" Cleo said.

"Let's all be silly together!"

Do You Remember?

Circle the right answer.

1. Clifford and his friends were playing . . .
    a. on a snowy hill.
    b. on the soccer field.
    c. at the playground.

2. What did Clifford make for Cleo?
    a. A snowman
    b. A snow couch
    c. A snowball

Which happened first?
Which happened next?
Which happened last?
Write a 1, 2, or 3 in the space after each sentence.

Cleo fell on the ice.   _____

T-Bone did his famous Hop,
Hop, and Slide.   _____

Clifford spun around and
around on his tail.   _____

Answers:

Clifford spun around and around on his tail. (3)
T-Bone did his famous Hop, Hop, and Slide. (1)
Cleo fell on the ice. (2)
2. b
1. b

Clifford THE BIG RED DOG ®
CLIFFORD'S LOOSE TOOTH

Adapted by Wendy Cheyette Lewison

Illustrated by John and Sandrina Kurtz

**Based on the Scholastic book series
"Clifford The Big Red Dog"
by Norman Bridwell**

Clifford was happy.

He had a nice big bone

to chew on.

All of a sudden,

he stopped chewing.

"Uh-oh," he said.

"My tooth is loose."

Clifford had never felt

a loose tooth before.

It wiggled.

It wobbled.

He was worried.

"Don't worry, Clifford,"

said Emily Elizabeth.

"It's just a loose puppy tooth.

When it falls out,

a new one will grow in its place."

"See?" said Emily Elizabeth.

"I have some new teeth!"

Emily Elizabeth went into the house.

She came out with a box.

In the box was a shiny quarter.

"The Tooth Fairy took my old tooth,"

said Emily Elizabeth.

"She left this for me

under my pillow."

Clifford looked at the beautiful,

shiny quarter.

Maybe he would get a treat

from the Tooth Fairy, too!

Off he went to tell
Cleo and T-Bone.

"Hmm," said Cleo.
"I bet we can help that
tooth along a little bit."

"How can we do that?"
asked Clifford.

"We can just pull it out!"
said Cleo.

"I don't think so…"
said Clifford.

"You could sneeze it out,"

said T-Bone.

"On the other hand…

Mrs. Bleakman might not

like that so much."

"Maybe you could chew
some bubble gum,"
said Cleo.

"A LOT of bubble gum.

Lots and lots and lots!"

Clifford thought about

chewing bubble gum.

He thought about the bubble

he would blow—

bigger and bigger and bigger.

Pop! went the bubble.

What a mess!

"Thank you for your ideas,"
Clifford said to his friends.

Then Clifford waited

for his tooth to come out

all by itself.

It was hard to wait.

But one day,

out it came!

That night, Clifford put

the tooth under his pillow.

Now everyone could see

Clifford's big tooth!

Do You Remember?

Circle the right answer.

1. When Clifford felt his loose tooth, he was chewing on…
   a. a bug.
   b. a bone.
   c. a ball.

2. Cleo and _____ thought of ways to help Clifford's tooth come out early.
   a. Mac
   b. Charley
   c. T-Bone

Which happened first?
Which happened next?
Which happened last?
Write a 1, 2, or 3 in the space after each sentence.

The Tooth Fairy gave Clifford a bone. _____

Emily Elizabeth showed Clifford her quarter. _____

Clifford imagined blowing a very big bubble. _____

Answers:

Clifford imagined blowing a very big bubble. (2)
Emily Elizabeth showed Clifford her quarter. (1)
The Tooth Fairy gave Clifford a bone. (3)
2. c
1. b

In the morning, Clifford

found a very big treat

from the Tooth Fairy…

who gave Clifford's tooth

to Mr. and Mrs. Howard

at The Sea Shell shop.